# Grimm's
## fairy tales

Illustrated By
## Greg Hildebrandt

The Unicorn Publishing House, Inc.
New Jersey

# Sleeping Beauty

There once lived a King and a Queen, who were childless. They had always wanted a child, but for a long time had none. Then one day, they happened upon a frog, who said, "Within one year, you shall have a child." And at the end of a year, a beautiful daughter was born.

The King called for a royal feast to be held. And what a grand feast it was. It seemed everyone in the kingdom was invited. Even the fairies were invited, that is, all except one. There was one fairy who was most wicked, and the King prayed she would not hear of the feast. But she did.

She appeared in a terrible rage, for in truth, she was angry and hurt that she was not invited. She placed a horrible curse upon the poor child, crying out, "When the Princess reaches her fifteenth birthday she shall prick herself on a spinning wheel and fall dead!" Without another word, the fairy vanished.

Everyone was horrified, but another fairy quickly stepped forward, saying, "Though I cannot break this wicked curse, I can soften it. The Princess shall not die, but will fall into a deep sleep that will last a hundred years."

The King was so fearful for his daughter's safety that he ordered all the spinning wheels in the kingdom to be gathered up and burned. As time went on, the Princess grew into a beautiful and thoughtful young woman.

Now it happened that on her fifteen birthday the King and Queen were away from home, leaving the Princess quite alone. She decided to take a walk through the castle that morning, and in a little room she found an old woman, busily working on a spinning wheel. "Good day, Granny," said the Princess. "What are you doing?"

"I am spinning, my child."

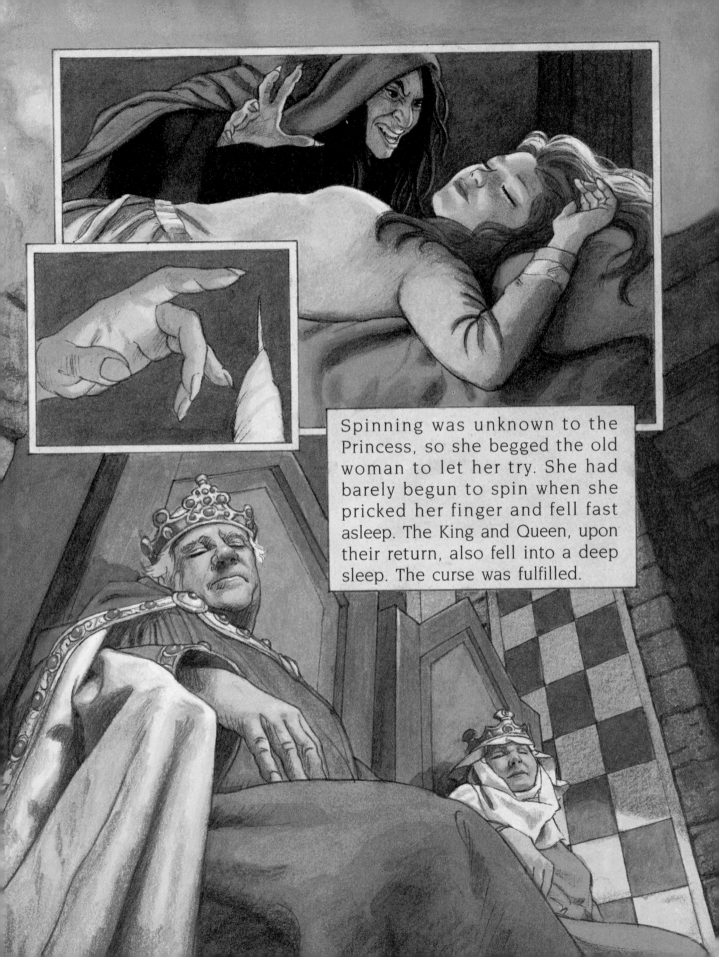

Spinning was unknown to the Princess, so she begged the old woman to let her try. She had barely begun to spin when she pricked her finger and fell fast asleep. The King and Queen, upon their return, also fell into a deep sleep. The curse was fulfilled.

In fact, everyone in the castle fell fast asleep. The evil fairy then cast a wicked spell and a huge hedge of briar roses grew up around the castle. The briars grew so high that they surrounded the castle like a fortess wall. As long as the Princess lay asleep, all were forbidden to enter lest the curse be broken.

But many tried—*and many failed*. The legend grew up in the land that there was a lovely Sleeping Beauty, Briar Rose, within the castle walls. Knights came from far and wide to try to rescue her. All soon found themselves lost or trapped in the briar hedge and died miserable deaths.

After many years had passed a young Prince came to the kingdom and heard the story of Sleeping Beauty. He determined he would try to save her. Now luckily, on the day he entered the briar hedge a hundred years had passed, and the Princess was to wake up that very morning. The hedge opened up before him as he made his way to the castle.

He entered the castle and found the King and Queen asleep on their thrones. The Prince searched throughout the castle, where he found the cook, the maids, and even the Princess' pet doves all fast asleep. At last he reached the room where the Princess was asleep.

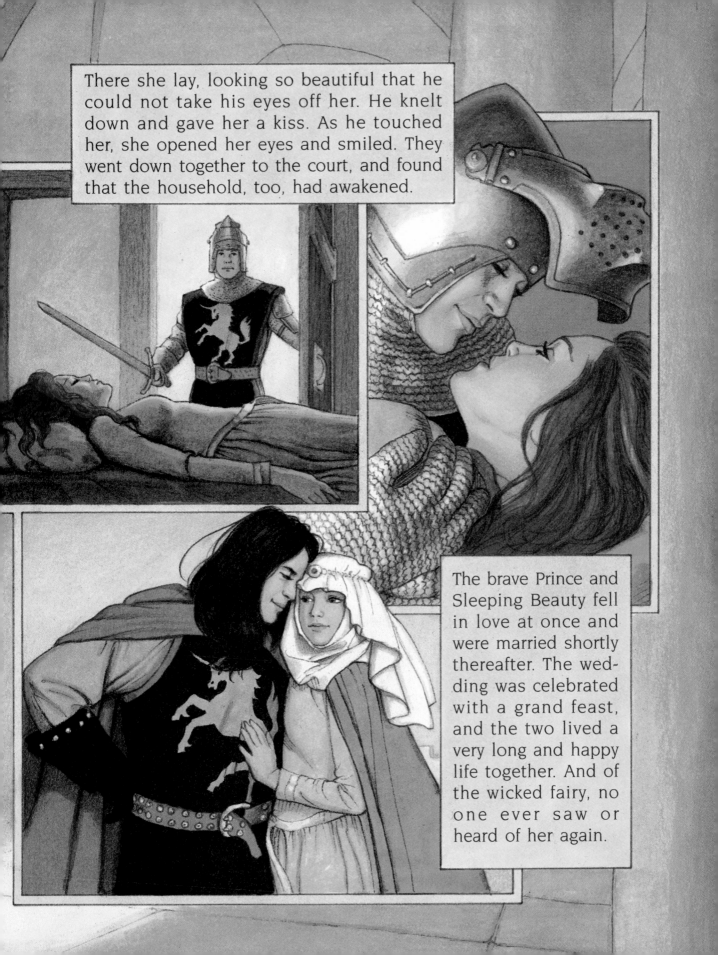

There she lay, looking so beautiful that he could not take his eyes off her. He knelt down and gave her a kiss. As he touched her, she opened her eyes and smiled. They went down together to the court, and found that the household, too, had awakened.

The brave Prince and Sleeping Beauty fell in love at once and were married shortly thereafter. The wedding was celebrated with a grand feast, and the two lived a very long and happy life together. And of the wicked fairy, no one ever saw or heard of her again.

# Rumpelstiltskin

There was once a poor miller who loved to boast. Now this miller had a beautiful daughter, and it happened one day that he spoke to the King. He lied, saying, "Sire, I have a daughter who can spin gold out of straw."

The King said, "Bring this clever girl to the castle tomorrow, so that I might see this miracle for myself." She arrived the next day, and the King took her to a room full of straw, and said, "If by first morning's light you have not spun this straw into gold, you shall surely die."

The poor girl sat and began to sob, for she didn't have the least idea of how to spin straw into gold. All at once there appeared a little man, who said, "Do not weep my child, for I can spin straw into gold! But if I do, what will you give me in return?"

"I will give you my neck-lace," she said, smiling. Taking the necklace, he sat down to his work.

He worked all night at the spinning wheel, and to the girl's amazement and delight, he indeed spun straw into gold. Just before morning he finished his magical work. With all the straw now spun into gold, he bid the girl good-day and left.

When the King returned that morning, he was delighted by the sight of a room full of gold. But he was not yet satisfied. He took the girl to a still larger room full of straw, and said, "If you value your life, spin this straw into gold by first morning's light, or you shall die." After the King left, she began to weep. But again the little man appeared.

"What will you give me if I spin the straw into gold for you?" he asked.
"I will give you the ring off my finger."
The little man agreed, and taking the ring, sat down and spun all the straw into gold.

The King was amazed to find another room full of gold. He took her quickly to a huge room full of straw, and said, "This last room of straw you must spin into gold in one night, but if you do you shall be my Queen and rule the whole kingdom by my side."

When she was alone the little man came again to her, saying, "If I spin the straw into gold, what will you give to me?"
"I have nothing left that I can give."

"Well then, you must promise me your first child if you become Queen! If you will promise me that, I will spin the straw into gold."

The girl thought it a silly demand and decided to promise the little man what he wanted, knowing full well she would never keep such a promise. The little man was satisfied, though, and spun the straw into gold.
The King *did* keep his promise, and married the miller's daughter at once. She became a Queen.

When a year had passed a daughter was born. The Queen had forgotten all about her promise to the little man. But he appeared one day before her at the castle.

"I have come for the child. Give her to me as you promised." The Queen began to weep and moan so that the little man finally said, "I will give you three days, and if you can tell me my name within that time you can keep the child." Then he left her.

When he came the next day, she tried every name she could think of, but every time he replied, "No, no, no, that's not my name. You now have but two days to guess my name."

The Queen sent her servants throughout the kingdom to find out who the little man was, but no one seemed to know him. "No, no, no, that's not my name. You have but one day for this guessing game."

The third day a servant returned, saying, "I found a little man last night singing by a fire deep in the woods. He sang, 'Today I bake and brew my beer./Tomorrow I bring the Queen's child here./Oh! lucky for me not a soul does know/That Rumpelstiltskin is my name. Ho! Ho!'" The Queen cried with joy upon hearing the name.

The little man arrived soon after, and the Queen politely asked, "Is your name Tom? No? Is it Harry? No? Is it Joseph? No?" And then with a little smile, she said, "Is it, by chance, Rumpelstiltskin?"

"The devil told you that! The devil told you that!" he screamed. "Unfair! Unfair!" And in a rage he stamped one foot down, then the other, and then both feet, till he went right through the floor and disappeared underground forever.

# Snow-White & Rose-Red

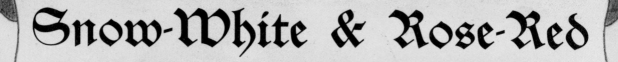

Once there was a poor widow who lived in a little hut with her two daughters. One girl was named Snow-White and the other was called Rose-Red, as they had been named after the flowers that grew around the cottage. They loved each other dearly and never parted.

Now it happened one cold and snowy winter night, a knock came at the door. Rose-Red opened the door, thinking it was some traveler needing shelter. She froze with fright at the sight of a huge bear.

The bear, however, spoke gently to her, saying, "Don't be afraid, I will not harm you. I am frozen and only wish to come in and warm myself." She led him to the warm fire and the two girls brushed the snow from his frosty coat.

From that night on they became the best of friends. The bear would often visit them, spending the night by the warm fire. But with the coming of spring, the bear said to them, "I must go away, and I cannot return the whole summer." Sadly, the girls waved good-bye."

One spring day, as the girls gathered wood in the forest, they came across a dwarf, who had caught his beard in a split tree. "What have you done to yourself, little man?" asked Snow-White.

"Foolish child!" said he. "Can't you see I caught my beard while splitting this log. Here it sticks and I cannot get away. Help me!" The girls thought hard of what to do.

They tried hard to pull the little man free, but his beard was caught too tightly in the log.
"Ouch! You cruel girls! You're killing me! Ouch!"

Then Rose-Red had an idea. She took a little knife and cut his beard free. "Stupid child! Oh, my beautiful beard! Curse you for your foolishness!" And the dwarf grabbed his sack of gold and left without one word of thanks.

Some weeks later they came across the dwarf again, this time with his beard caught in a fishing line. "Oh, don't just stand there fools, help me before the fish pulls me into the water!" he cried with rage.

Rose-Red took her knife out and clipped his beard free once more. "No, no! What have you done, you dumb child! My lovely beard! Gone! Gone!" Taking up a sack of pearls, he left all in a huff.

Not many days after, they saw the rude little man again in the forest. As he walked along, a giant eagle swooped down and grabbed him up. The girls ran to him at once and held tight to his legs lest he be carried away and eaten. The eagle struggled to lift the dwarf, but at last it released its grip and the little man came tumbling down to the ground.

He should have been thankful to the girls for saving his life, but the ungrateful dwarf only screamed, "Could you not have treated me more gently? Look! my coat is torn! You are both meddling fools!" And he threw a sack of precious stones over his shoulder and left without another word.

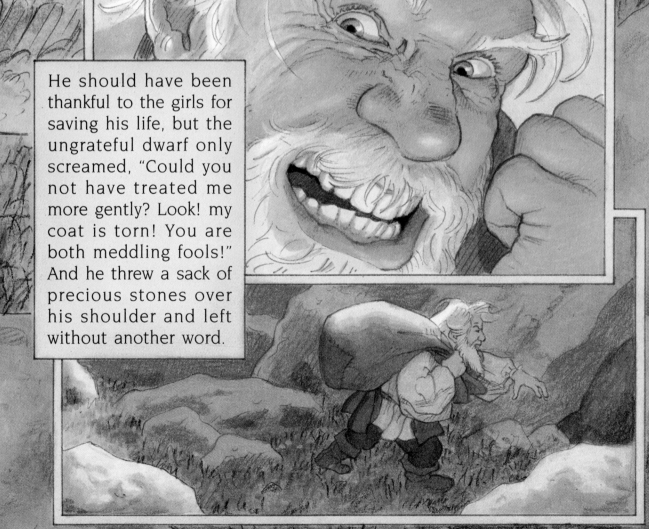

Later that same day, the girls saw the dwarf deep in the wood, drooling over his treasures. Spotting them, he cried, "Why are you here? Do you think to steal my treasure, you wicked girls?" At that moment, the great bear appeared, and the dwarf trembled with fear, saying, "Spare me, my lord, do not kill me!" But the bear did just that.

The girls stood amazed as they saw the furry coat of the bear fall off, and a handsome prince now stood before them, and said, "Do not fear, for you see, that wicked dwarf cast a spell on me to steal my riches." And the three hugged, and were dear friends for life.

# Red Riding Hood

Once upon a time there was a sweet little girl whom everybody loved. But most of all, she was loved by her grandmother. She had once given the little girl a red velvet cloak. The little girl loved it so much she would never wear anything else. And that is how she became known as Little Red Riding Hood.

One day her mother called to her, "Take these jellies and jams to Grandmother. She is not feeling well, and they will cheer her. And when you get there, don't forget to say 'Good morning,' and to be very polite."

Now her grandmother lived far in the woods, so Red Riding Hood set off at once. It wasn't long, though, before she met a Wolf. Red Riding Hood didn't know what a wicked fellow he was, so, of course, she wasn't a bit afraid.

"Good morning, Red Riding Hood," the Wolf said prettily.

"Good morning, Wolf," Red Riding Hood said.

"May I walk with you?" asked the Wolf. "Where are you off to, my child?"
"Come, walk with me, Wolf, for I am going to my grandmother's house far in the woods."
They walked together for a while when the Wolf had the wicked idea he would go ahead of her and eat the Grandmother, then wait for Red Riding Hood to come later and gobble her up also. He told the little girl she should pick pretty flowers as a present.

While the little girl picked pretty flowers in a field, the Wolf snuck off and made straightaway for the Grandmother's house. He knocked at the door, and he heard a voice say, "Red Riding Hood? Come, come in, my child."

He entered the cottage and ate the Grandmother up. Then he put some of her bedclothes on and climbed into bed to wait for Red Riding Hood. When the little girl had picked enough flowers, she set off again for her Grandmother's house. Once there, she found the door wide open.

She went inside, and said, "Good morning, Grandmother." But she heard no reply. Coming closer, she said, "Oh, Grandmother, what big ears you have." "The better to hear you with, my dear."

"Grandmother, what big eyes you have," she said.
"The better to see you with, my dear," said the Wolf.
"What big hands you have, Grandmother."
"The better to catch hold of you with, my dear," said the Wolf, moving a bit closer.

"But Grandmother, what big teeth you have."
"The better to eat you up with, my dear."
Hardly had the Wolf said this than he jumped out of bed and swallowed poor Little Red Riding Hood up in one bite. Now the Wolf was very satisfied indeed, being so full, so he went back to the bed and laid down. Soon he was snoring loudly.

A hunter came passing by the Grandmother's house and stopped. "How loudly the old woman is snoring," he thought. "I should go and see if she is in any trouble.

Climbing up the hill to the house, the noble hunter knocked at the door, but he received no reply.

He entered quietly, and finding no one in the room, made his way to the bed. The bed curtains were drawn, but the deafening sound of snoring could be heard.

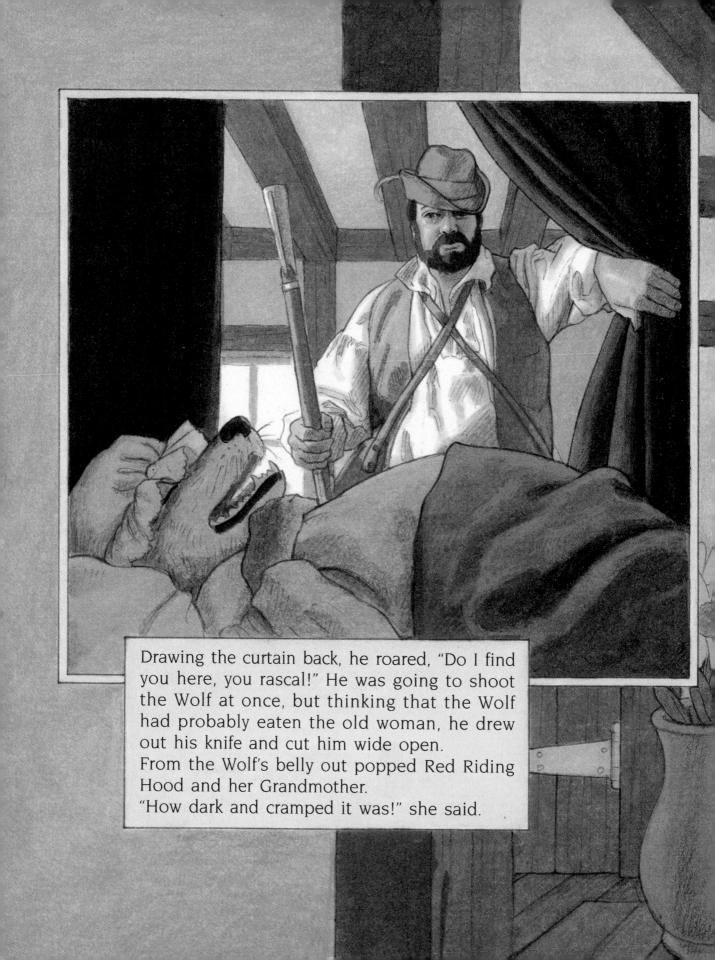

Drawing the curtain back, he roared, "Do I find you here, you rascal!" He was going to shoot the Wolf at once, but thinking that the Wolf had probably eaten the old woman, he drew out his knife and cut him wide open.
From the Wolf's belly out popped Red Riding Hood and her Grandmother.
"How dark and cramped it was!" she said.

The hunter took the dead wolf away and Red Riding Hood finally had her visit with her Grandmother. They ate cake and cookies and had a very happy time together. On her way back home, Red Riding Hood thought to herself, "I will never again wander off into the woods by myself, and never, oh never, will I talk to a Wolf!"